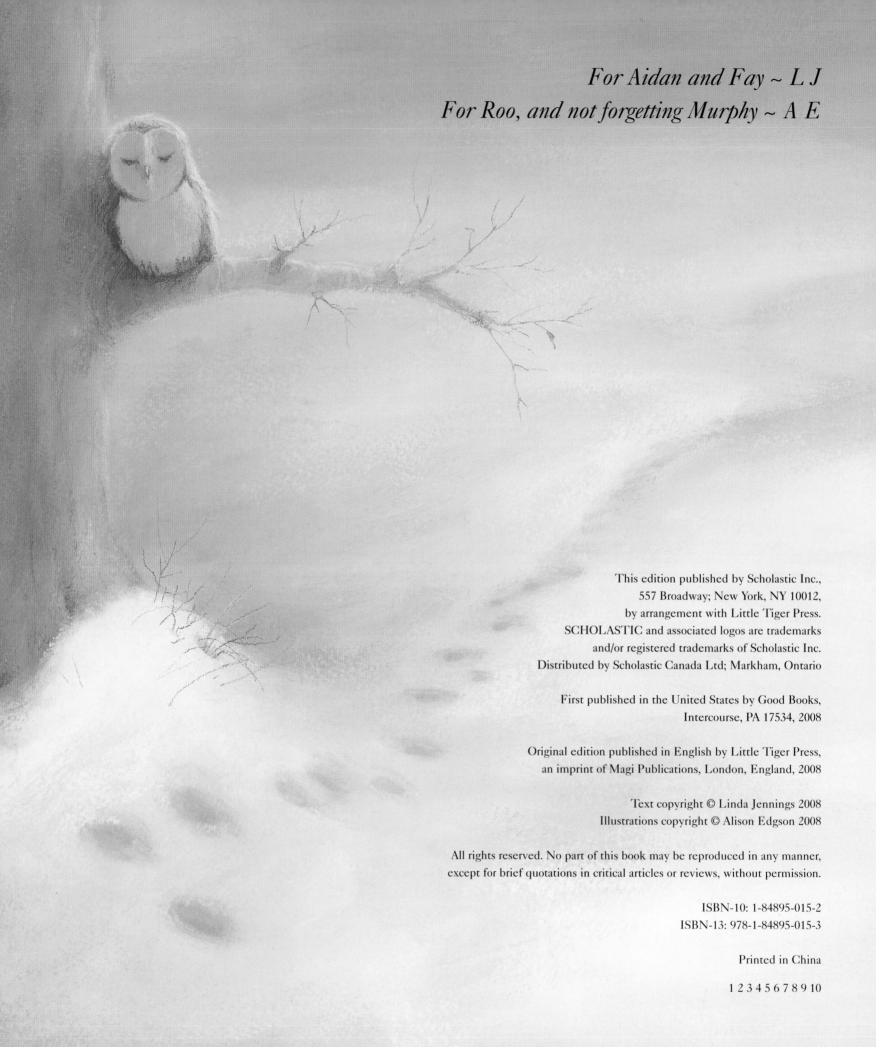

For Aidan and Fay ~ L J
For Roo, and not forgetting Murphy ~ A E

This edition published by Scholastic Inc.,
557 Broadway; New York, NY 10012,
by arrangement with Little Tiger Press.
SCHOLASTIC and associated logos are trademarks
and/or registered trademarks of Scholastic Inc.
Distributed by Scholastic Canada Ltd; Markham, Ontario

First published in the United States by Good Books,
Intercourse, PA 17534, 2008

Original edition published in English by Little Tiger Press,
an imprint of Magi Publications, London, England, 2008

Text copyright © Linda Jennings 2008
Illustrations copyright © Alison Edgson 2008

ISBN-10: 1-84895-015-2
ISBN-13: 978-1-84895-015-3

Printed in China

1 2 3 4 5 6 7 8 9 10

Lost in the Snow

Linda Jennings

illustrated by Alison Edgson

Ollie peeped out of the barn door. Something cold and wet plopped on his nose. "What's all this white stuff, Mom?" he squeaked. "Can we eat it?"

"It's snow, Ollie," his mom laughed. "It falls like rain in winter. And no, you shouldn't eat it."

"Can we play in it, then?" he asked.

"Please, Mom?" cried Sheba and Sam.

"Of course you can," said Mom, "but don't go too far."

Sam and Sheba skidded and slid
across the icy farmyard.
"Wait for me!" yelped Ollie,
racing after them.

When the puppies reached
the field, they stopped and stared.
There was snow everywhere.
"Let's play!" cried Ollie.

The puppies chased and dug
and rolled under the flying
snowflakes, until
suddenly . . .

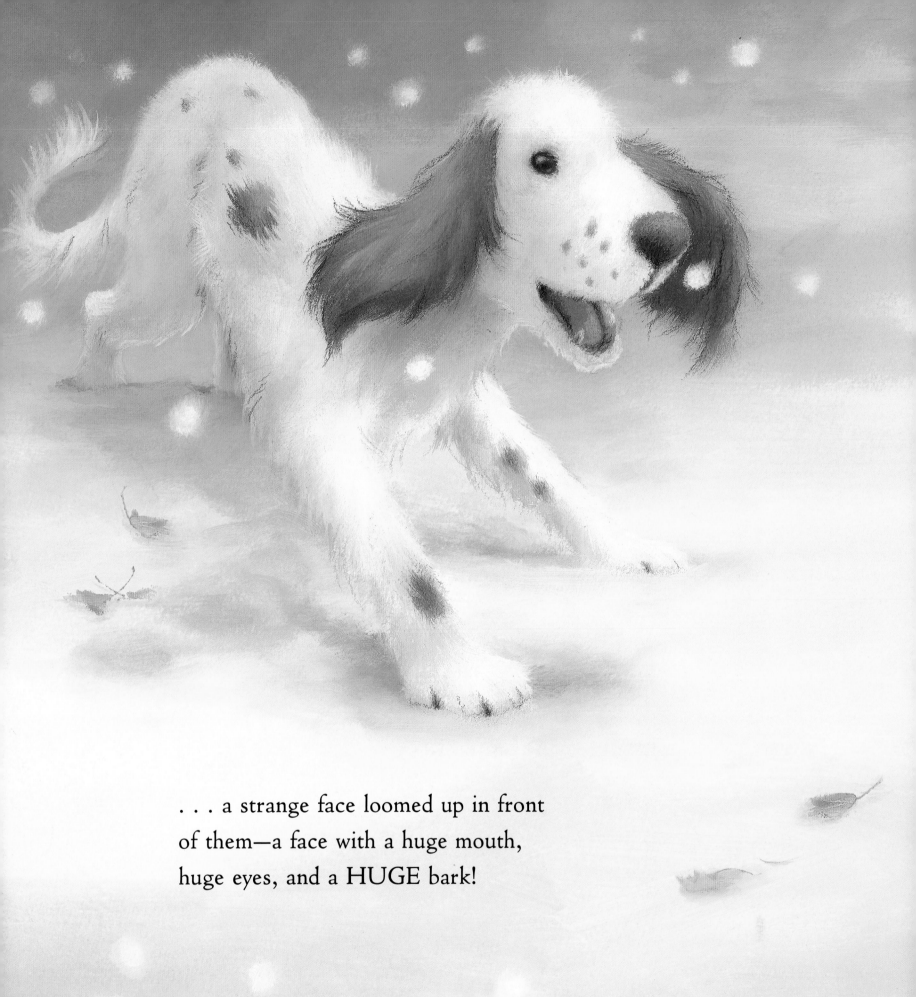

. . . a strange face loomed up in front
of them—a face with a huge mouth,
huge eyes, and a HUGE bark!

For a moment, the puppies
froze with fear.
"RUN!" Sheba cried.

The puppies rushed off through the flurrying snowflakes. Ollie's paws scrabbled and skidded as he ran and ran, until at last the dog's barks faded and everything was quiet and still. But where were Sheba and Sam? Where were the farmyard and barn?

"Oh no," whimpered Ollie.
"I'm lost!"

"Too whit,

too whoo,

who are you?"

hooted a voice high above him. Ollie looked up. Two big, round eyes stared down.

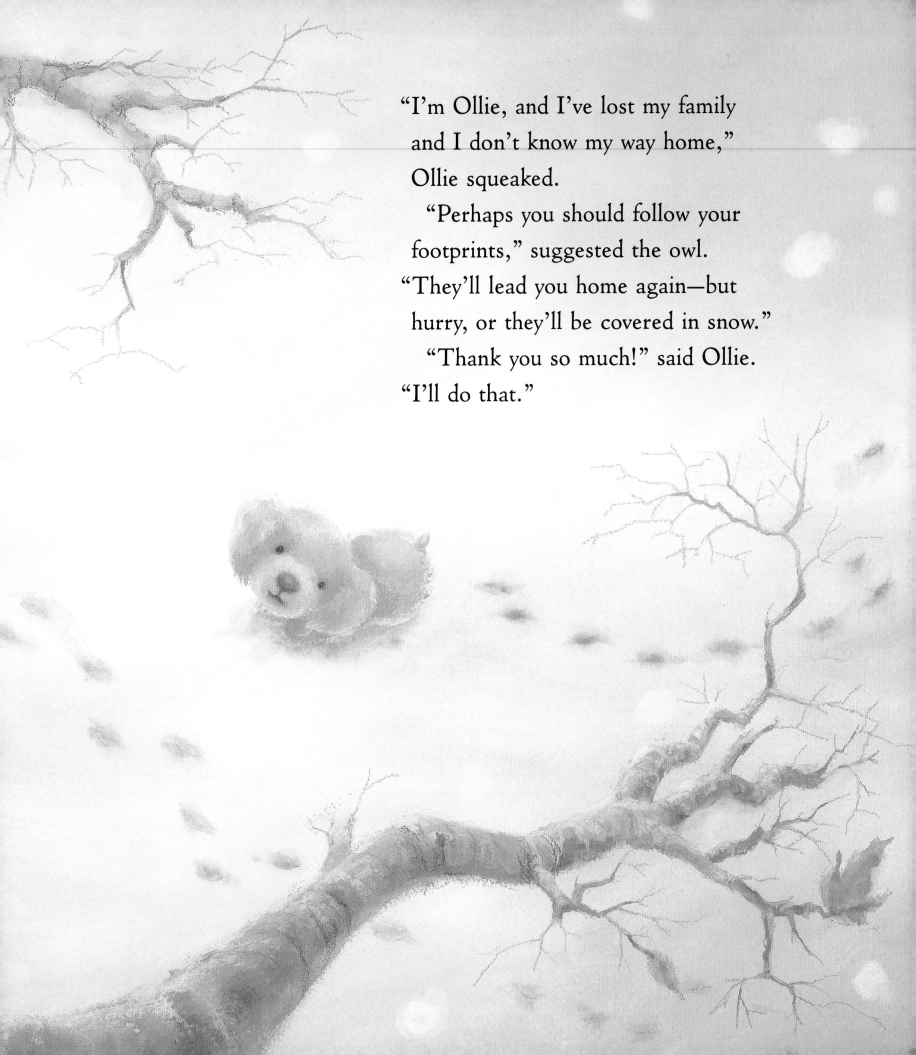

"I'm Ollie, and I've lost my family
and I don't know my way home,"
Ollie squeaked.

"Perhaps you should follow your
footprints," suggested the owl.
"They'll lead you home again—but
hurry, or they'll be covered in snow."

"Thank you so much!" said Ollie.
"I'll do that."

Tail wagging, he set off. But by the time he reached the middle of the field, the footprints were disappearing under fresh snow. Soon, Ollie couldn't see them at all.

He trudged on and on as the snow grew deeper. "I must keep going," he panted. "I *must* get back to my nice warm home and supper."

At last, Ollie reached the edge of the woods. Were these the woods by his farm? If they were, then he was almost home!

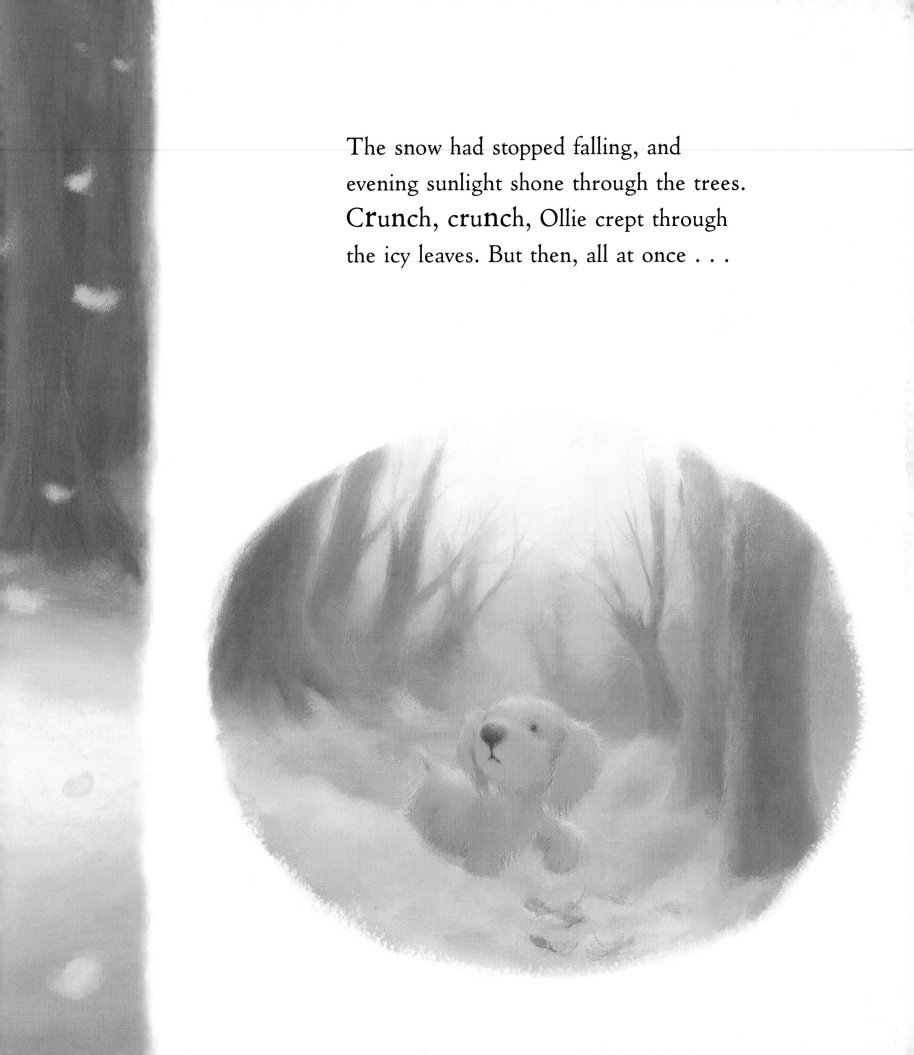

The snow had stopped falling, and
evening sunlight shone through the trees.
Crunch, crunch, Ollie crept through
the icy leaves. But then, all at once . . .

Swoosh!

Ollie slipped down
an icy slope,

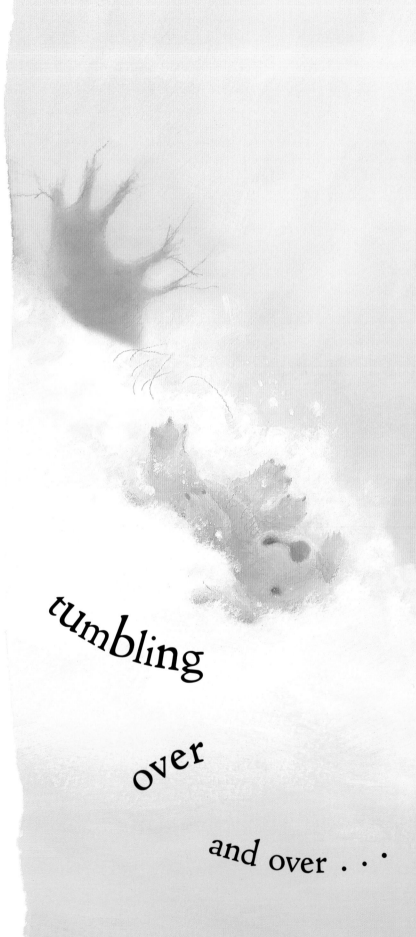

tumbling

over

and over . . .

THUMP!

From the shadow of the bushes, three fox cubs stared out at him.

"Look what the snow's blown in," said one.

"What a runt!" said another.

"This is *our* home," said the third. "Go away!"

"But I don't know which way to go!" cried Ollie. Sadly he walked away. He would have to find his own way home.

Ollie reached the edge of the woods, but he still couldn't see the farm. He tried to cheer himself up. He'd have so much to tell Sam and Sheba when he got home!

But the snow was falling again, thicker and faster. As he struggled on, Ollie began to think he would never see his family again.

Cold, hungry, and very, very tired, Ollie crawled under a bush.

A mouse scurried past his feet and disappeared into a small hole. "I wish I could find somewhere safe and warm to sleep, too," Ollie sighed. But as he closed his eyes, he heard something . . .

"Ollie! OLLIE! Where are you?"
 Ollie peeked out from the bush—
it was Mom!

"Mom! Sam! Sheba! I'm over here!"
And across the frozen field, Ollie
raced to meet them.

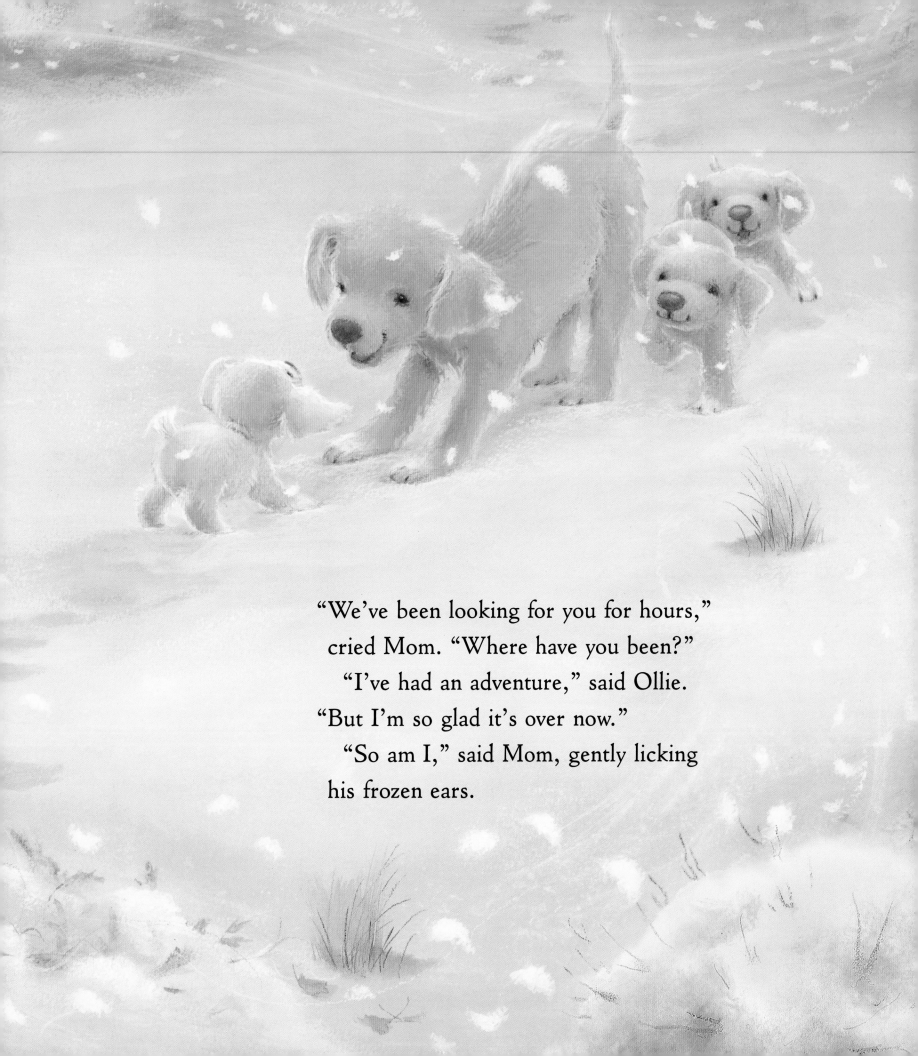

"We've been looking for you for hours,"
cried Mom. "Where have you been?"
"I've had an adventure," said Ollie.
"But I'm so glad it's over now."
"So am I," said Mom, gently licking
his frozen ears.

Home at last, Ollie curled up with his brother and sister in their cozy bed. The puppies wanted to know all about Ollie's big adventure.

"Tell us more about the owl!" cried Sheba.

"And the nasty fox cubs!" squeaked Sam.

But, warm and snug, his tummy full of dinner, Ollie fell fast asleep. His story would have to wait for another time.